www.enchantedlion.com

First English–language edition, published in 2022 by Enchanted Lion Books
248 Creamer Street, Studio 4, Brooklyn, NY 11231
First published in Italy as A sbagliare le storie
Original Italian edition published by Edizione EL
Text taken from Favole al telefono by Gianni Rodari, 1962
Italian–language text copyright © 1980 by Maria Ferretti Rodari and Paola Rodari
English–language translation copyright © 2020 by Antony Shugaar
Illustrations copyright © 2020 by Beatrice Alemagna
Photo of Beatrice Alemagna © Joséphine de Rohan–Chabot
Graphic design by Chialab
All rights reserved under International and Pan–American Copyright Conventions
A CIP is on record with the Library of Congress
ISBN 978–1–59270–360–9
Printed in Italy by Società Editoriale Grafiche AZ

First Printing

TELLING STORIES WRONG
GIANNI RODARI

Illustrated by
BEATRICE ALEMAGNA

Translated from Italian by
ANTONY SHUGAAR

Enchanted Lion Books
NEW YORK

"Once upon a time, there was a girl who was called Little Yellow Riding Hood."

"No, red!"

"Oh, right! Little Red Riding Hood. Her mother called her one day and said: Listen, Little Green Riding Hood..."

"No, Red!"

"Oh, right! Red.

Her mother said: Now go to Aunt Hildegard's house
and take her this potato peel."

"No, it's: Go to your grandmother's house and bring her this warm loaf of bread."

"Oh, right! So the little girl went into the woods,

and that's where she met a giraffe."

"Oh, right! And the wolf asked her:
How much is six times eight?"

"Not even close, Grandpa! The wolf
asked her: Where are you going?"

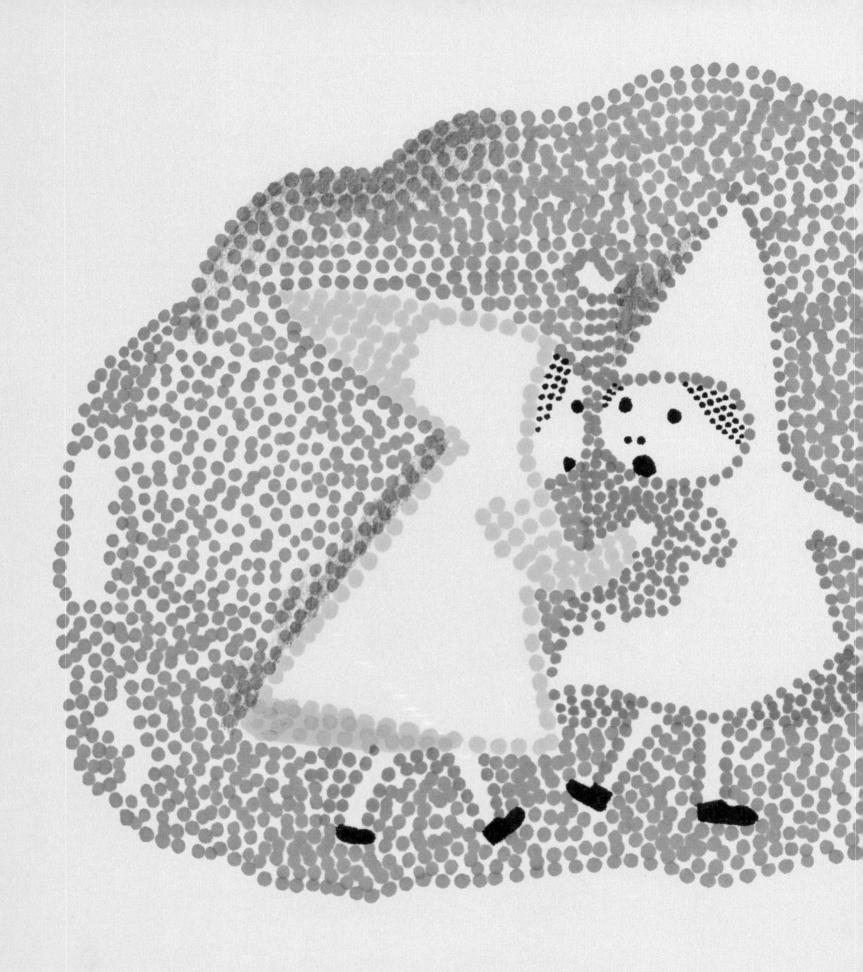

"Oh, right! And Little Black Riding Hood answered ..."

"It was Little Red Riding Hood! Red! Red! Red!"

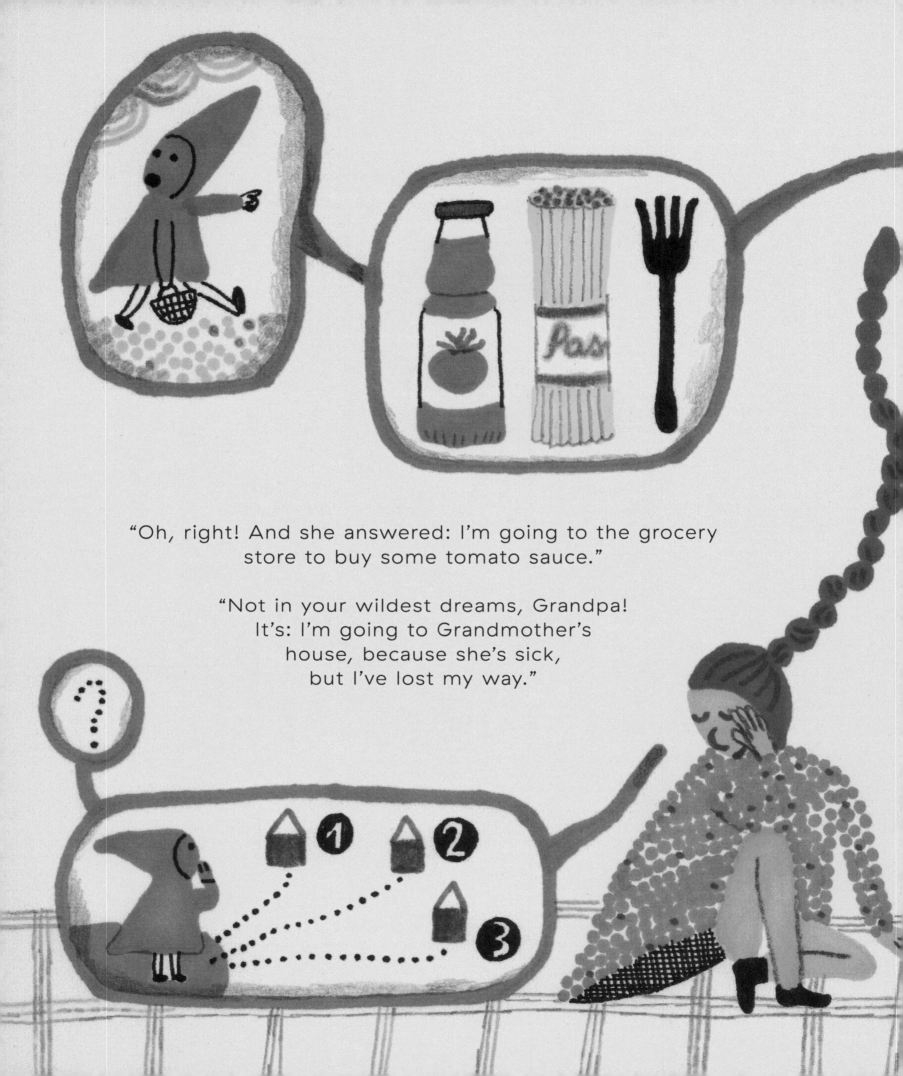

"Oh, right! And she answered: I'm going to the grocery store to buy some tomato sauce."

"Not in your wildest dreams, Grandpa! It's: I'm going to Grandmother's house, because she's sick, but I've lost my way."

"Oh, right! So the horse said to her..."

"What horse, Grandpa? It was a wolf."

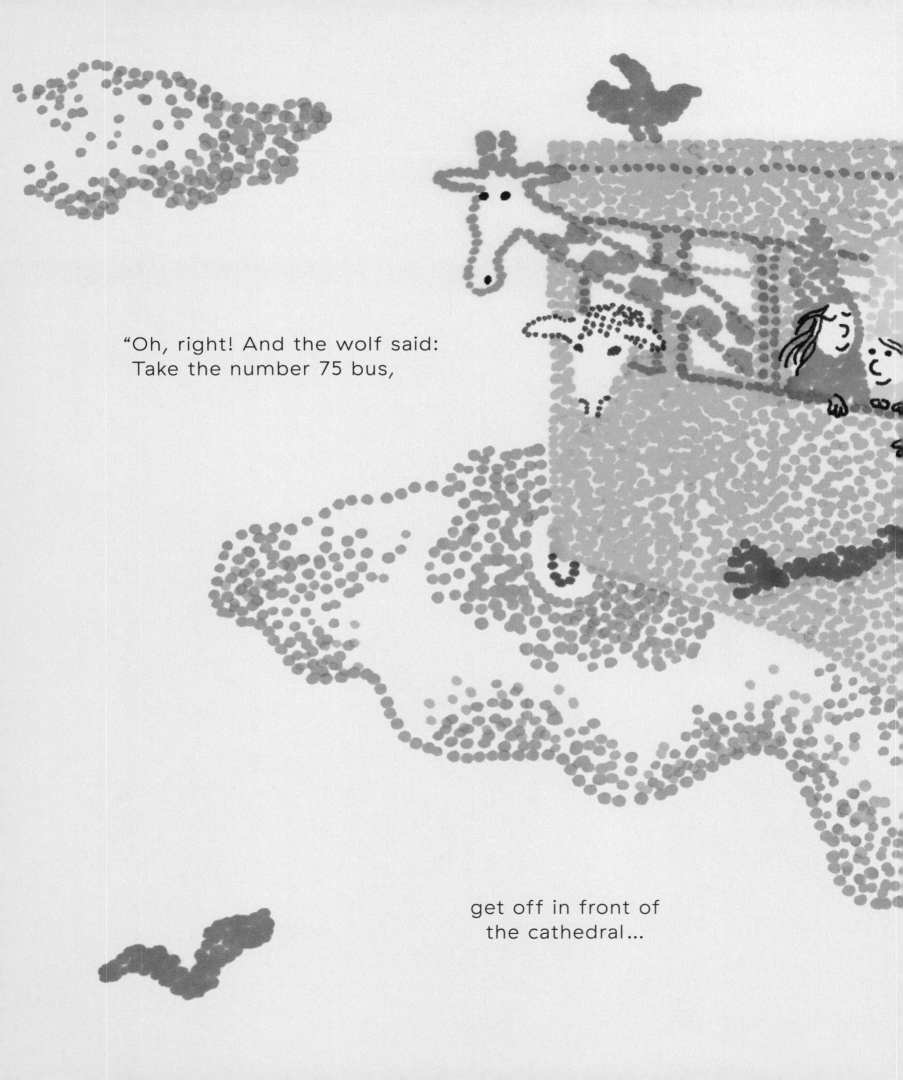

"Oh, right! And the wolf said:
Take the number 75 bus,

get off in front of
the cathedral...

turn right, and there you'll find three steps and a quarter on the ground. Forget about the three steps, pick up the quarter, and go buy yourself some bubble gum."

"Grandpa, you really don't know how to tell a story. You get everything wrong. But all the same, can I have a quarter to buy some bubble gum?"

"Sure you can. Here you go."

And Grandpa went back to reading his newspaper.

GIANNI RODARI

Gianni Rodari was born in Omegna, Italy in 1920. After finishing high school with a teaching certificate, he taught elementary school for several years. After the end of World War II, he began working as a journalist, writing for such Socialist newspapers as *L'Unità*, *Pioniere*, and *Paese Sera*. In the 1950s, he began to write and publish children's books, winning acclaim and popularity: poetry, wordplay, and later on, fables and novels that explore themes of freedom, justice, dignity, civic responsibility, and play with a lighthearted touch and seriousness of purpose. His books *The Adventures of Cipollino*, *Gelsomino in the Land of Liars*, *Nursery Rhymes in Heaven and on Earth*, *Telephone Tales*, and *The Book of Mistakes*, to name just a few, have been translated into many languages. In 1970, he received the Hans Christian Andersen Award, widely considered the Nobel Prize of children's literature. In the 1960s and 1970s, Rodari also engaged intensely "in the field," attending pedagogical conferences and meetings with teachers, librarians, parents, and students. This work led him to write *The Grammar of Fantasy*, an enduring text and lodestar for those who see critical thinking and imaginative freedom as central to human liberation and justice. Rodari died in Rome in 1980, at the age of just fifty-nine. In 2020, the centennial of his birth was celebrated, providing an opportunity to reflect on his stature as a thinker, the importance of his writings, his farsighted views on education, and his delight in narrative itself.

BEATRICE ALEMAGNA

Beatrice Alemagna was born in Bologna in 1973. After studying editorial graphics at the Higher Institute for Artistic Industries (ISIA) in Urbino, she moved to Paris and began a career as an author and illustrator, first in France, and later internationally.

Beatrice has created posters for the Centre Pompidou in Paris and has been nominated for major awards in various countries, including the Astrid Lindgren Memorial Award (nominated six years running) and the Hans Christian Andersen Award. Her illustrations have been featured in many exhibitions, from Munich and Paris to Italy, Japan, and the US, and she has received numerous awards for her work. She has illustrated the work of such authors as David Grossmann, Ágota Kristóf, Raymond Queneau, Aldous Huxley, Guillaume Apollinaire, David Almond, Astrid Lindgren, and, of course, Gianni Rodari, whom she considers one of her "spiritual fathers." Her previous two books with Enchanted Lion have been *Child of Glass* and *The Wonderful Fluffy Little Squishy*.

"Telling Stories Wrong" originally appeared in *Telephone Tales*, one of the most well-known and well-loved of Gianni Rodari's books. Composed of many stories within a story, each of the narratives of *Telephone Tales* is set in a different place and time, with unconventional characters and a wonderful mix of reality and fantasy.